It's Time for Preschool!

ESMÉ RAJI CODELL

It's Time for Preschool!

ILLUSTRATED BY **SUE RAMÁ**

Greenwillow Books, *An Imprint of HarperCollinsPublishers*

The artist would like to thank Diane Morton and the staff of The School for Young Children
at Saint Joseph College for inspiring her with the beauty and sweetness of their school.

Library of Congress Cataloging-in-Publication Data:
Codell, Esmé Raji, (date). It's time for preschool! / Esmé Raji Codell ; illustrated by Sue Ramá.
p. cm. "Greenwillow Books."
ISBN 978-0-06-145518-6 (trade ed.) — ISBN 978-0-06-145519-3 (lib. bdg.) [1. Education, Preschool—Juvenile literature.
2. Preschool children—Juvenile literature. 3. First day of school—Juvenile literature.]
I. Ramá, Sue, ill. II. Title.   LB1140.2C645 2012   372.21—dc23   2011033582
12 13 14 15 16 SCP 10 9 8 7 6 5 4 3 2 1   First Edition

 Greenwillow Books

In memory and admiration of the lives
and work of Fred Rogers and Josie Carey—E.R.C.

Dedicated, with much gratitude, to Matthew Kaufman,
and also to David Raymond and Jessica Glass,
who taught me the pleasures of bottle-feeding lambs—S.R.

Can't wait! School's great!

All the big kids go.

You grew. School's new.

Many things to know.

What's at home? What's at school?

What's different, what's the same?

Let's go to a preschool room

and see what we can name.

Preschool Time!

When you walk in the door,
who will you see?

Friends,

teachers,

helpers,

maybe a class pet.

Explore the room!

MRS. MAYA

Max

ALEXA

Potty,

cubby,

name tag.

By the end of the first day,

you will know where

all of the important things are.

Time to Play

Sand table, water table,

dress-up clothes,

beads to string.

Make a store with a
cash register that rings.

Look at a book.

Tell a story with a puppet.

Cook some pretend food . . .

or maybe some real food!

We can play we are princesses,

or the police, or animals in the zoo.

Or maybe we can pretend we are dinosaurs. *Roar!*

Or princess dinosaurs, or police dinosaurs, or . . .

Whoops!

The teacher says it's circle time.

We stop whatever we are doing right away!

We can finish later.

Now it's time to gather together

with the whole class.

Say the alphabet, count to ten.

Show-and-tell, or sing a song.

When it's time to talk together,

circle time's where we belong.

Circle
Time

R S T U V W X Y Z

JOBS

Who is sick, and who brought snack?

Who gets to pass the papers back?

What's the weather? Who is new?

The teacher tells us what to do.

Sitting cross-legged on the floor,

we all say good morning,

and learn what's in store.

Sometimes during circle time,

we talk about what time of year it is.

What time of year is it when you see a pumpkin?

Or a snowflake?

Or a flower?

Spring, summer, winter, fall,

we celebrate seasons and holidays.

Happy everything to all!

Circle time is just one special time

we have at preschool.

There is also snack time, when we eat.

And story time, when we listen.

And nap time, when we rest.

But every time is . . .

Sharing Time

Share a box of raisins.

Share a box of crayons.

Share a box of building blocks
(though you had other plans).

Share a great idea you have
by raising up your hand.

You can share some drums and bells
to make a marching band.

Share cupcakes on your birthday.

Don't make teacher tell you twice.

Sharing isn't always fun,

but it is always nice.

Manners

Sharing is one kind of manners.

Manners are things we do and say

to show people that we care about them

and know that they are in the world.

Excuse mes and *thank yous* and *sorrys*

and *pleases*.

We wipe noses with tissues

and wash hands after sneezes.

(This keeps friends and teachers from catching diseases.)
Sometimes we forget. That's okay.
We'll get other chances to remember and be kind through the day.

Fire Drill

Sometimes we think about what to do in an emergency.

The fire drill is when we practice our best safety choices.

We all get in line and we don't use our voices.

We take a little walk around the block.

A loud noise is ringing, like a big alarm clock.

Sometimes the fire truck comes around.

How exciting! How noisy! We are safe and sound.

Thinking-about-Home Time

Even though you are busy, sometimes

you think about Mom or Dad

or Grandma or Grandpa

or someone who loves you

and takes care of you

and how they are not at preschool.

That might be a wobbly time,

or a worrying time,

or a wondering time.

But it is a very short time.

WHAT IS MOMMY DOING RIGHT NOW WHILE I AM AT SCHOOL?

What is Mommy doing?
Is she going to the store?
Is she using the computer?
Is she cleaning up the floor?

What is Daddy doing?
Is he driving in his van?
Is he taking care of baby?
Is he cooking in a pan?

Are they sitting at a desk or
are they talking on the phone?
What are the grown-ups doing
when the grown-ups are alone?

What are the grown-ups doing?
They are doing what they do.
Preschool is *your* doing time,
and you are busy, too.
We think about each other
as we work and as we play
and know that we will see each other
later in the day.

Time for Friends

Here, have half a cracker!

That's what friends do.

Give a hug. Take a hug.

Give one back.

Come sit by me!

Hold hands.

That way, everyone

can see we are friends.

Friends use words.

Sometimes we even

talk at the same time.

We can sing together,

too. Real loud!

LA LA LAAA!

And then we can be quiet as mice.

See, we can switch it!

LOUD! Quiet. LOUD! Quiet.

Maybe later, maybe come over,

maybe today, maybe another time.

The playing doesn't have to end.

Not when you make a friend.

Go go go! We use our bodies.

Brrom! Beep-beep! Waooooo!

The teacher looks tired.

That's how we know we

are having a great day.

That's also how we know

it is almost nap time.

Shhhhh! It's time to rest on cots and mats.

The room is dark (but not too dark),

and grown-ups are nearby,

still working in the room.

Nap Time

If we can't fall asleep, that's fine.

We just close our eyes

and slow down for a little while,

and think of quiet, restful, happy things.

Field Trip Time

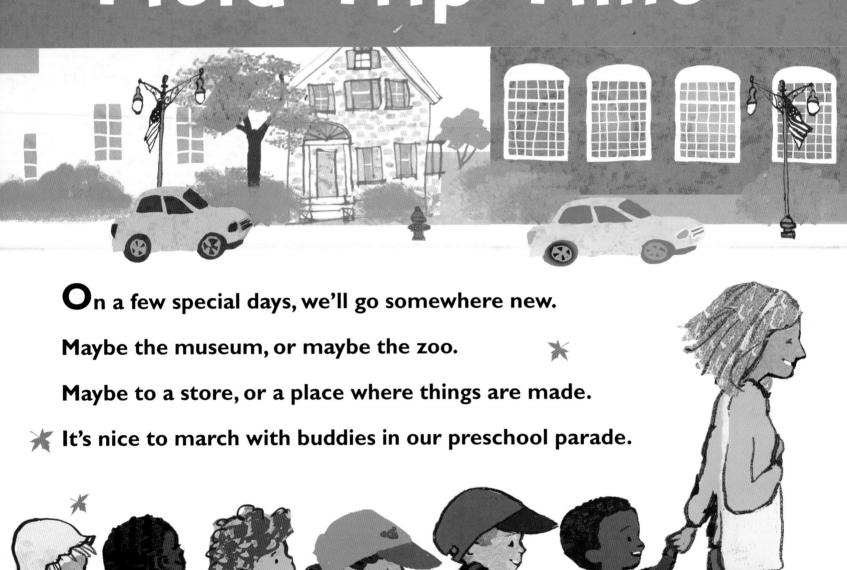

On a few special days, we'll go somewhere new.

Maybe the museum, or maybe the zoo.

Maybe to a store, or a place where things are made.

It's nice to march with buddies in our preschool parade.

Time to Make Stuff

Crayons, scissors, paint, and glue,

sometimes clay and glitter, too.

The sky can be green, the grass can be blue—

whatever you make is up to you.

No two works of art are ever the same.

When it's done and it's dry, you can add your name.

Then your work will be hung on a fridge or a door.

And YES, you can make a dinosaur.

Clean-up Time

Clean up, clean up,

it's time to clean up!

Time to put away toys

and books

and bells

and blocks

and cars

and crackers

and crayons

and clay

and all of the parts of our wonderful day.

Time to put on our boots and our jackets.

Time to check our cubbies

for artwork and envelopes

that our teacher wants us to take home.

Home! That is where we are going

at the end of our preschool day.

DON'T WORRY

Never never never

In a thousand million years

Would Mom or Dad not pick you up,

So let that ease your fears.

A dad might lose track of the time,

A sitter might be tardy,

A mom might run a little late

departing from a party,

But never never never

(I will say it with a shout)

Would your folks forget to pick you up.

It's not even worth thinking about.

You're done, school's fun!

Tomorrow's a new day

of counting, art, and alphabet,

and play and play and play.

Time to Go Home!

What's at home? What's at school?

In both places, children grow.

In both places, grown-ups love them . . .

more than children ever know.

Preparing for
Preschool!
HINTS FOR PARENTS

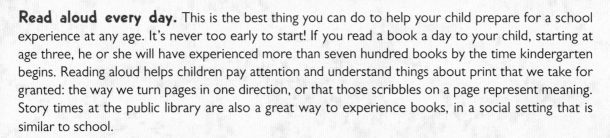

Read aloud every day. This is the best thing you can do to help your child prepare for a school experience at any age. It's never too early to start! If you read a book a day to your child, starting at age three, he or she will have experienced more than seven hundred books by the time kindergarten begins. Reading aloud helps children pay attention and understand things about print that we take for granted: the way we turn pages in one direction, or that those scribbles on a page represent meaning. Story times at the public library are also a great way to experience books, in a social setting that is similar to school.

Let children help. Slow down and let children try to stir, fold, sweep, sort, wash, and put things away. Feeling like a helper builds self-esteem and independence and creates a connection to family and community. It is also a great way to practice tactile and large-motor skills that will help children in playing, cooking, and crafting in preschool.

Connect with nature. Take walks, and talk about what you experience using all the senses: the sight of clouds in the sky, the smell of autumn leaves, the cold feeling of hands in mittens. Count the petals on a flower, take care of a pet, water a plant, collect rocks or shells, touch the rough bark of a tree, splash in a puddle. Talk about how things come about and the way things work. Pick things up and notice together: there are patterns and colors and things to count everywhere in the natural world. A sense of structure and cycles is reassuring to a young child (and to us all), and can foster a calmness and curiosity that will help with future transitions.

Relax. It is easy as a parent to feel anxious or competitive about finding a preschool. There may be inner conflicts about having to work, or worries about whether half-day or full-day preschool experiences are best. Good-byes are hard for both parent and child. Visiting the space ahead of time and creating a friendly rapport with the teacher will put you and your preschooler at greater ease. But trust that all is well, that the details and decisions that seem so monumental right now will grow smaller with distance, and most of all, that your child has resilience, courage, empathy, imagination, and ability yet to be revealed . . . in preschool!